To Cami~~l~~la and Gianna,

Sorry I misspelled your name Camila - Aunty E corrected me!

Hope you enjoy this book!

Love

Grandma Stitches

This book is in honor of the wonderfully diverse individuals and families served by Tammy Lynn Center, and the incredible staff who nurtures and cares for them.

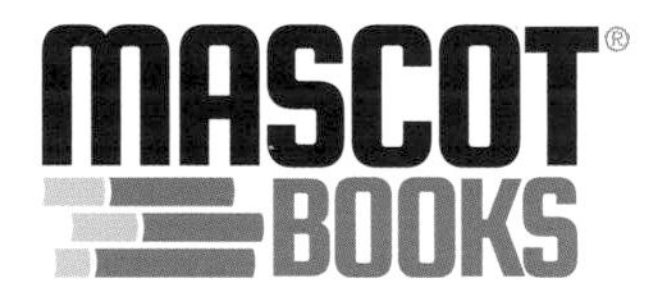

www.mascotbooks.com

We Are Not the Same, and That's Okay

For more information, please contact:
Mascot Books
620 Herndon Parkway #320
Herndon, VA 20170
info@mascotbooks.com

Library of Congress Control Number: 2019900629

CPSIA Code: PRT1019A
ISBN-13: 978-1-64307-236-4

Printed in the United States

We Are Not the Same, and That's Okay

Written by Amanda Lamb
Illustrated by Gabriela Christine

Some people have blue eyes, and some have red **hair**.
Some people are brown, and some are **fair**.

We are not the same, and that's **okay**.
We are each unique and special in our own **way**.

When we see someone who looks different, it can be scary at first. We don't always know what to say or how to act. But if we take a little time to learn about the person, we might find out we're not that different after all.

Anna sits in a special chair that helps keep her head up and her back straight. Anna doesn't talk, which might be different than you and me.

Anna's friends help her get around her school in her special chair. They help her eat and they move her from her chair to her bed when she gets tired. Sometimes, she is fussy when she doesn't get her way, just like most kids.

But if you sit with Anna, you'll learn she likes the same things that you do: playing with her friends, going outside, and reading books. She looks at people with her eyes that are as blue as the ocean. She might even want to hold your hand to show you how much she likes you. If you're lucky, she'll smile at you with her entire face. If you're extremely lucky, you might get to hear her laugh from deep down in her belly.

How do you show people you like them?

Sometimes, a new person you meet may look like you but not act like you. Joshua can run and jump and play with a ball, but he doesn't have the words to tell you what he's thinking. His brain works differently than ours, but his heart is the same.

Special therapists are helping him learn how to make words.

Sometimes, Joshua gets upset because he thinks that no one can understand him. But the therapists do understand Joshua, even when he doesn't speak. They know him so well they can tell what he's thinking and feeling. They make him feel safe.

Have you ever felt like no one understands you?

People who are different can be kids, or they can be grown-ups. Charlie is a grown-up, but he acts like a kid. He is sweet and playful. He likes baseball and fire trucks and has a great big heart.

Charlie lives with his friends at a very special place built just for them. He has a mother and father and sisters and brothers at home who visit him often, but he is also part of the family here. Charlie likes to go on field trips to the fire station where the firefighters let him spray the hose.

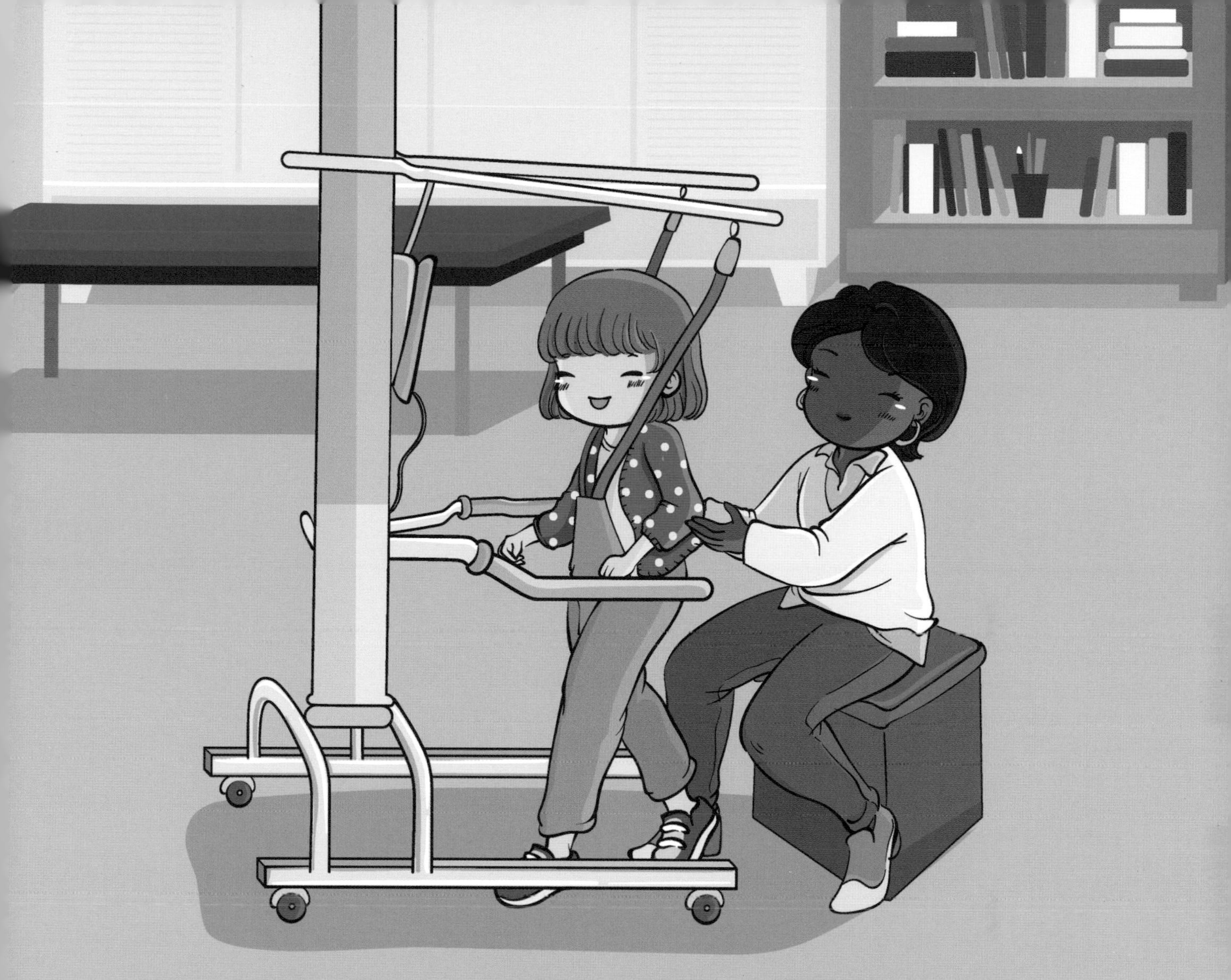

Anna, Joshua, and Charlie all learn and grow at a place where they're loved and safe. In their community, it's okay to be different.

Sometimes, the kids in their community use special equipment, like a tube to help them breathe or eat, or something to help them move, like leg braces, walkers, or wheelchairs.

Have you ever needed help with something?

Here, Anna, Joshua, and Charlie have special friends who support and love them. It feels like a magical place.

In this special place, hugs are frequent and free, given out like candy on Halloween. Happiness is always in the air, and smiles are easy to find. It is a place where anything seems possible.

Just like how some kids have blue eyes and some have brown eyes, Anna, Joshua, and Charlie were born with differences that make them special and unique.

We shouldn't shy away from people because they are different. We should embrace them for who they are, just like we want others to embrace us for who we are.

So if you see Anna, Joshua, or Charlie, don't stare at them or walk away. Stop and sit for a while. Hold Anna's hand, throw a ball with Joshua, or show Charlie your toy fire truck.

We are not the same, and that's **okay**.
We can still all learn how to **play**.

If you see someone **new**,
someone who doesn't look like **you**,
reach out and make a **friend**.
Do that, and your smiles will never **end**.